MW00618342

KLAUN

(clown)

Jesper the Klaun
& Lenore Watts
Illustrated by Francesco Orazzini

Authors:
Jesper the Klaun
Lenore Watts

Illustrator:
Francesco Orazzini
www.francesco-orazzini.com

Editor/Art Director: Joseph Benner
Assistant Editor: Steve Knight

Publisher: Scope Publishing LLC
Contact: scopepublishing@gmail.com

Website: **www.klaunclownstory.com**
Social media: **@jespertheklaun**

ISBN: 978-1-7351412-0-6

Contents

Note to Reader:

Many of today's clowning customs—the red nose, face-paint, etc.—can be traced back to an ancient tribe of nomadic entertainers known as the Klaun. The members of this clan have guarded their secret lineage for centuries while hiding in plain sight throughout the world. This book contains *The Story of The Klaun*, an origin story covertly passed down to the youth of each Klaun generation. Until recently, this story has only been shared with descendants of the Klaun.

Prologue

My name is Lenore Watts. I go by Lenny. Once upon a time, I was a successful journalist, but now I mostly just drink, smoke, and steal wallets and phones off of suits. I'm thirty tomorrow. Almost broke. Sick and tired all the time.

Not exactly sure how I ended up like this, but completely sure it's my own fault. I guess it is worth mentioning though that when I was a kid, I saw my dad get strangled to death. So there's that. There's always that. And Mom passed a few months back, so that's about it for family. The last bright idea I had to make an honest living, a self-published newsmagazine, flickered out a few weeks ago when the advertisers stopped buying. Since then I've just been back to picking pockets and drinking away the cash. Dulling the senses. Trying to forget who I am.

Slumped on a barstool in Brooklyn at mid-afternoon again, I'm nursing my liquor along with the other casualties at the usual dive. The old bartender flips through an old newspaper. There's no chit-chat. The windows were blacked out long ago, and aside from a few fluorescent lights, we're blanketed in merciful darkness.

The door creaks and we all cringe from the cruel light. When I look up, I find what appears to be a giant bearded hobo in a long shabby coat on the stool next to mine. His proximity irks me for a moment. There are plenty of other seats. I am considering whether to say something or just change stools when he turns to me. There is an unnerving intensity in his gaze. Finally, he says, "You run a local newspaper. You're a reporter."

I'm a bit thrown for a second, but quickly figure he's seen me around town or even in that very bar selling ad space to the owner. I've got no idea what he's after, but ok… "Yeah, well… it's just online now. No more print copies, just the website." There's not really a website, but whatever. "You know how it is, everything's online these days."

The massive stranger then gets up and nods to the bartender, who without a word sets down two rocks glasses and a bottle of their best Scotch whiskey. He grabs it and says to me, "I've got a story for you. Leave everything here." Then he walks round the end of the bar and exits through the saloon-style swinging doors that lead to an unused backroom.

I take a minute to finish off what's left of my drink and collect my thoughts. I have no idea who this guy is or what he wants, but I do know he's got a full bottle of Glenfiddich and something serious to tell me. He seems to think I'm still a journalist, so who knows? Maybe it's a scoop I can sell to a news outlet and turn into some decent cash. But this guy feels like the type who's dangerous just to know. And I know the type. So it's a bad idea. I'll walk away.

Then again, he does have that bottle of scotch. So I hit start on my cellphone's audio recorder and head through the swinging doors. In the dimly lit backroom, there is a small abandoned stage cluttered with empty boxes, trash, and dusty equipment. He's sitting in the furthest corner at a small table next to the stage, back against the wall. "You call me Jesper" he rasps, and I pull up a chair across from him.

He fills both of our glasses, slugs his down and refills it. I raise my own glass and awkwardly offer a "Cheers," which he ignores aside from a slight grunt. He is slowly shifting his gaze between his glass, the door, and me. It's then I realize that he's situated himself to monitor the doorway. Clearly this is a mistake. I grab my glass, take a gulp, and set my phone on the table to record.

The following is a transcript of that recording.

Jesper: His eyes flash toward the doors again before he whispers, *"You remember that little kid that went missing, 'bout two years back? The little rich girl from Crown Heights? That disappeared from that street fair?"*

Lenny: *"I think so, yeah. The blonde one, right? Yeah, sure."*

Jesper: *"And you remember how the kid's body was left on the parents' doorstep? And when the cops finally found the son of a bitch who'd done it, he'd already been beaten to death?"*

Lenny: *"Yeah, and they thought maybe the father was the one who had killed him, but they never figured it out, right? Yeah, sure, I remember all that. Why?"*

Jesper: *"Well, I can tell you for a fact it was not that child's father who put that animal down."*

Lenny: *"Ok, so who was it then? You think you know who…"* I catch Jesper's cold stare and realize this is a stupid question.

Jesper: *"By the time I'd finally tracked him down, it was too late. He'd probably just killed the poor girl just moments before I got there. I was too late. I'd planned to make my killin' him look like a suicide, but when I saw the kid, well …everything went red,* *ya know? Shit. So anyway, once I was done with him, I wrapped her as carefully as I could and I left her outside her family's home. The cops and the media all thought the murderer had set the girl's body outside her parents' home to taunt them or something. And that's how they took it. And for that, I'm sorry. I regret that. I dunno, maybe I shoulda left a note or something. I dunno. But I'm sorry about that. I didn't mean to upset them. My intention was just to get them their daughter's body back. And with all the security cameras, I couldn't leave her at the hospital, so I just figured..."*

Lenny: *"Ok, so hold on. Wait a second."* This guy is hard to follow and my head is already spinning. *"What are you saying? You knew who'd kidnapped that girl, so you went after the guy? By yourself? Why not just go to the police?"*

Jesper: Suddenly agitated, he scoffs, *"Hmmff... Yeah, sure, the cops. That's a great idea. They'd just start roundin' up all sortsa clowns even though most of them've got absolutely no clue about any of this. And actually, no, I had no idea about that girl till I got there. But see, this is what I do, kid... I hunt. I was already tracking down that piece of shit off a previous murder."* Jesper then mutters something inaudible.

Lenny: *"What? Sorry, what was that?"*

Jesper: He doesn't hear me. Just keeps muttering to himself. Then he shoots back his drink, refills our glasses and continues. He's looking toward me, but not quite at me as he speaks. *"I'm gonna catch Hell for this from both sides."* He looks down and rubs a colorful handwoven bracelet on his wrist. It's one of those friendship bracelets, the type that school kids make.

Lenny: *"Catch Hell for what?"*

Jesper: *"For telling you our story."* He sighs heavily. *"But it's outta control, and we've gotta tell people about clowns. There's just no gettin' round it anymore. Hell, the… they've already broken the code a thousand times anyway, I'm sure of that. People already know about us. And all of a sudden we might lose this war, and badly. We're too outnumbered. So we gotta do something. We've got to warn people. Before it's too late."*

That's twice now he's mentioned clowns. At first I'd assumed it was just an expression. But now it sinks in as I notice traces of white makeup caked deep into his wrinkles and stuck at the roots of his beard and eyebrows.

Lenny: *"So, hold on a second. What's gotten out of control? What war are you talking about? And what are you telling me you're an actual clown or something?"*

Jesper: Stares down at his drink. *"With a 'K'. It's Klaun. K-L-A-U-N. And it's time for the world to know our story. It's time for the people to know about clowns."*

Jesper drops silent and stares vacantly at his glass. He is somewhere between solemn and sullen as several minutes quietly pass. I'm at a loss. So, I flip my phone over on the table and reveal that we are recording - that we've been recording, and I slide the microphone part a bit closer to him.

He glares at the recorder, then at me. But suddenly softens as he looks down and fiddles with that bracelet again. Just as quickly he stiffens again and neither blinks nor breathes. He catches me off guard when he suddenly blurts out:

Jesper: *"They eat them. They eat the kids."*

Lenny: *"What? What are you talking about? Who eats kids?"*

Jesper leans away, cocks his head back, and squints down his nose at me. One of the barflies stumbles through the swinging doors to use the bathroom and Jesper abruptly returns to his drink, alternatively taking sips and staring blankly down at the table. It's like an illness washes over him, and I get the feeling he is going to get up to leave. But as soon as the guy exits the bathroom and is out of sight, Jesper continues.

Jesper: *"They cannibalize people... especially children."* He rubs that bracelet again. *"Innocent children for God's sake."*

I'm speechless. I finish off my drink, and somewhat brazenly grab the bottle and refill my glass. All I can do is stare at him and look for some sign that he's putting me on. But I can't shake the feeling this is no joke.

Jesper: *"I know. It sounds crazy. But when you know our story, when you know about Klaun history, you'll get a better grasp of it all and it starts to make more sense."*

Lenny: *"Ok, well..."*

Jesper: *"Alright, so, I decided the best way to tell you about the Klaun, at least to start, is to tell you the same way it was first told to me when I was a kid. So I brought this."* He reaches into one of the deep pockets of his black coat. *"See there's this old folktale in Klaun culture that's passed down from generation to generation."* He holds up what looks like a small leather-bound journal and carefully places it on the table. *"It's told to every Klaun child on the eve of their tenth birthday as a kind of bedtime story. But the thing is, it's more history than*

10

fiction, ya see. So I guess "folktale" is kinda the wrong word for it. But it's told like one, ya know? 'Cause it's for kids, to inform them about their secret heritage and also to sorta prime them, so to speak, for the uh, unusual lives let's just say, that they'll have to face as Klaun. It's an initiation really. Then they wake up the next morning on their birthday and it all begins."

Lenny: *"What begins?"*

Jesper: *"Everything. Learning what it is to be Klaun and preparing for it. Training. Joining the fold."*

We both take another swig. Then I gently pick up the bottle, top off Jesper's glass, and nod toward the notebook. Jesper leans forward, breathes deep, and slowly opens *The Story of the Klaun.*

Note to Reader:

The following is a transcript of Jesper the Klaun telling the story of his people's secret history and cultural origins. No substantive changes have been made to this transcript, but with Jesper's approval, a few minor grammar adjustments have been made for clarity.

The Story of the Klaun

Chapter I

During the Dark Ages, a colorful tribe of nomads traveled amongst the Forest Realms uplifting the spirits of whomever they met along their route. They were a cheerful clan of entertainers known as the Klaun. Physical expression came naturally to every Klaun and they spontaneously danced, flipped and cartwheeled through their days. An active, jubilant people with bright smiles and kind hearts, the Klaun were full of beauty and love.

The Klaun had sparkling eyes, fair skin, and round cherubic little noses that would turn bright pink with exercise or chilly weather. To the Klaun, the pink nose was a sign of health and vigor. Thus, they would sometimes adorn the tips of their noses with a single dab of red paste to express their vitality.

Lenny: *"So, wait… That's how the whole clown nose thing got started? That's where it comes from?"*

Jesper: His eyes dance as he looks up at me. *"Oh, we're just getting started, kid."*

The Klaun made and wore simple but well-tailored clothing accented with dashes of color. Many would garnish their hair with wildflowers. For special celebrations and ceremonies, some

Klaun donned a distinctive three-pronged hat, each prong representing one of *The Three Precepts of the Klaun*: Freedom, Kindness, and Cheer. The tribe's credo was, "Be well and merry!"

As the caravan of performers arrived at the outskirts of each village along their migratory route, they would cease travel and quickly erect a plethora of brightly colored tents and canopies. Soon, a wealth of tantalizing sights, sounds and smells emanated from the area, luring local inhabitants to come explore the famous Klaun Carnival.

The Klaun were renowned for their wildly fun celebrations, and the inhabitants of each land always looked forward to their return. Within each village, little boys and girls would leap with joy upon spotting the colorful wagons. "The Klaun! The Klaun! The carnival is HERE!" children would shout as they bounded to retrieve their parents and tug them toward the fun.

Carnival music filled the air as enraptured visitors joined the festivities. They were delighted at every turn by the Klaun's acrobatics, juggling, and silly magic shows. While enjoying the theatricalities of their hosts, carnival-goers could munch on candied apples, spiced-fig treats, nuts, and berries. Many Klaun also made and sold beautiful garments, marionettes, crafts and baubles. And a few times throughout the day, the crowds would be directed toward the largest tent for the more spectacular performances, where Klaun troupes performed elaborate skits combining physical comedy with stunt riding on horesback and magic tricks. At the end of each visit, each family was so blissfully infected by the contagious merriment of the Klaun that they would skip and dance together all the way back to their homes.

Chapter II

And so the Klaun tribe rambled happily along through kingdoms and seasons, attaining provisions and lighting their audiences' hearts with joy. But all along, far to the south of the Forest Realms, a dark storm was gathering. There, a lavish priest-king adorned with jewels and gold proclaimed he was chosen by "The One True God." This was a vengeful and angry god, and the Priest-King claimed that this god spoke to him directly, revealing Divine Will to him alone.

This tyrant commanded his ever growing army to conquer the surrounding empires, announcing, "Subjects! Our Lord, God, has honored me, His most humble servant, with sacred instructions. 'Tis the order of our Lord that we, His people, spread His Sacred Word and Holy Dominion far and wide!" The Priest-King's "Holy-Royal Army" ruthlessly complied as they captured, tortured and killed anyone who refused to obey the Priest-King and worship his god.

With unrelenting violence, the Priest-King conquered kingdom after kingdom, pushing the borders of his rule across the lands. Years passed in this way and his dominion grew ever greater. In time, his Holy-Royal Army encroached upon the kingdoms of the Forest Realms. Scores of brave citizens took up weapons and joined their kings'

armies, making valiant efforts to defend their homes and families. But they were quickly vanquished.

Soon the first kingdom of the Forest Realms was conquered. Survivors living under the Priest-King's rule had their spiritual and cultural traditions outlawed or appropriated as he sought to replace their identities with his religion. Traditional music was banned and instruments were smashed. Religious scripts were burned, spiritual totems confiscated, and places of worship destroyed. Conservative codes of conduct and dress, particularly for females, were enforced with brutality.

The Klaun tribe were panicked by the invasion and looked for guidance from their two leaders—a pair of half-brothers known as Jobo and Flecky. The pair were born of different Klaun mothers and were far apart in age, and neither of them had ever known their shared father, who was not of the clan. This fatherlessness had always pained Jobo, so when Flecky was born, Jobo vowed to fill that roll for his baby brother. The half-brothers were very close, but also quite different. Flecky was impulsive and charismatic, while Jobo was more contemplative and introverted. Together they struck a balance which served the tribe well.

Flecky believed the Klaun should respond to the Priest-King's invasion by joining one of the Forest Realms' armies in battle. But the gentler Jobo, wishing to keep his people from harm, explained, "We are a peaceful tribe, Fleck. We know almost nothing of real violence. No, no… this time will pass. Eventually the Kings of the Realms will unite and these invaders will retreat. Seasons always change. In the meantime, the best thing for our clan is to stay true to who we are. We will reroute our travels away from the besieged areas and stay within the free lands. We shall continue to perform. Now, more than ever, we must bring cheer and hope to the villagers."

Though a bit of a ruffian, Flecky was fiercely loyal to his older brother and trusted his judgement. So as he had always done, he worked in concert with Jobo to keep the clan united. Flecky was very persuasive - a boisterous, overbearing but charming rascal with a big toothy smile. He made the rounds that night, and soon had all of the clan feeling rallied and hopeful about Jobo's plan.

But wherever the Klaun caravan traveled, word of the encroaching Holy-Royal Army's savagery had so filled the people's hearts with dread that they were no longer captivated by the Klaun's antics. Before long, only a few separate parts of the Forest Realms remained free, cutting off the Klaun's migratory path. The two chiefs knew that their tribe had to retreat deep into the forest. "Brothers and sisters, take heart," Flecky told the tribe, "for Jobo has had another vision! We shall retain our freedom tucked safely within the trees until this scourge passes."

The Klaun were no strangers to the woods, but it had been generations since they needed to survive primarily off the land. As the popularity of their performances had grown over the years, they had become more and more able to acquire all they needed from the provincial markets. Now though, all of their food had to be hunted and foraged. It was a perilous struggle fraught with hungry predators, poisonous plants, and dark forest spirits. But with Jobo's wisdom and Flecky's goading, the Klaun were able to adapt, making homes in the forest within their carnival tents.

But the Klaun's notoriety throughout the Forest Realms was their undoing, for word eventually reached the Priest-King that a band of nomads had been evading his authority. The tyrant was incensed, but the Klaun's reputation as performers intrigued him as a way to entertain his court, so he sent scouting parties into the forests to locate the hidden tribe.

After searching for several days, a trio of scouts finally located the Klaun encampment. "Who is in charge here? We demand that whoever leads this clan step forth immediately!" the head scout shouted, and Jobo and Flecky stepped forward. The scout barked at them, "All of the clan is to surrender at once and you both are to be taken to our Lord's palace, whereupon you shall vow allegiance to the Priest-King and The One True God."

Flecky, frightened and outraged, spoke out for the entire clan and refused the royal order. He could not imagine that any Klaun would ever surrender their freedom. "A Klaun without freedom ceases to *be* Klaun at all! Without the Three Precepts, a Klaun does not exist! To betray the first of these?! To relinquish our freedom?! That would be the end of us!"

Jobo firmly supported his brother, "The Klaun have always sought peace, but we shall never submit to such tyranny. We shall never kneel to your so-called Lord!" The whole tribe erupted into cheers of support.

The scouts returned to the palace and relayed the message to the Priest-King. Irate to hear of the Klaun's defiance, he immediately declared them heretics and dispatched infantry to kill or capture the entire tribe.

Chapter III

Taking up arms was completely foreign to the Klaun. Merriment and goodwill had always been at the core of Klaun culture. The ways of war were unknown to them, and even the idea of killing a fellow human being was horrifying. But the decision had been made. The brothers had incited the clan, and now all were inflated with hubris. They would fight. The Klaun tribe, for the very first time, would become warriors.

The Priest-King's soldiers would be upon them within a matter of days. In need of a strategy, Jobo sealed himself away in his tent. When he finally emerged, Flecky gathered the tribe to hear their wise leader's vision. "Klaun warriors! Hear me!" Jobo called. "This battle is ours. To reach us, the invaders will have little choice but to travel along the Great River at the base of the ravine. It is there that we shall time our attack from the high ground. It is there that we shall CRUSH the enslavers and retain our FREEDOM!"

The warriors roared in support, and then Jobo lowered his voice and continued, "But that shall not be our only advantage, oh no. To bolster our strength, we shall call upon vengeful spirits to join us. It is well known that specters of the murdered are doomed to wander the earth until their deaths are avenged. It is the only way to disentangle themselves from this world. And so, first we shall use chalk to whiten our skin to the pallor of corpses, and then we shall summon the spirits of the Holy Army's victims to enter our bodies and EMPOWER us with their fury! To finally exact their revenge and gain their liberation, these desperate souls are sure to oblige. Together we ALL shall find salvation through this battle!"

Flecky spouted, "Ah HAAAAH! And SO! When the Priest-King's murderous soldiers, those death mongers, come for us, they will realize their FATE! They will cower in repentance as their nightmares come true and a vengeful army of the dead is unleashed upon them!"

"Ooofah!" the Klaun warriors cheered, "OOOFAAAH!!!"

Although emboldened by this plan and committed to victory, each warrior solemnly reflected on the end of the Klaun tribe's peaceful existence as they applied their war paint and prepared for battle. To make their undead army even more bizarre, many Klaun dyed, stretched and glued their wiry hair straight out, creating a frightful appearance. They wore mismatched garments and some donned the three-pronged hat. All of the warriors covered their skin with corpse makeup and adorned their noses with the clan's customary spot of red.

For weapons, the Klaun made do with what was at hand: clubs, shovels, scythes, knives, chains, spikes, hammers, poles, saws, and axes.

Though traditionally peaceful, they were a physically formidable tribe. Their life of travel and acrobatics had made them strong and agile. With little effort, they quickly learned how to wield their weapons.

Based upon what they had heard about the Klaun's peaceful nature, the Holy-Royal troops anticipated little to no resistance. But they were not to meet the sweet-tempered Klaun described in the stories of the villagers who adored them. Threatened with mortal violence, and with nowhere to run or hide, the formerly gentle travelers had turned desperate and vicious.

Chapter IV

The Klaun remained vigilant with posted sentinels, and late one night they sighted the incoming soldiers. As dawn approached, the Holy-Royal troops arrived between the riverbank and a steep hill where the painted warriors were lying in wait. As the Klaun peered through the waning darkness, the roar of the powerful river filled their ears as they muttered spells for the ghosts of the Priest-King's victims to inhabit them.

Dawn tinged the sky and the Klaun stealthily rose and advanced over the ridge and through the shadows, quickening their pace with each step. They reached full speed, weapons raised, just as the sun broke behind them. Chains whirling overhead, axes and hammers hoisted and cocked, the possessed killers burst out with cackles of frenzied laughter and descended upon their victims.

"GWAAHahaaaah!" — *THWAK!*

"HAH hah!"—*SPLAT!*

"Keekeh YEEEheeheeeee!!!"

They maniacally crushed bones and sliced flesh as the petrified soldiers tried to comprehend the deathly creatures attacking them.

"OH MY GAH!"—*CRRAACK!*

"AAAAAGH, NO, PLEASE!"—*SLAASH!*

"BAAAH hah, HEH! HEE HEE HEEEEEEEE!!!"

The cacophony of laughter and screams reached a fever pitch as the Klaun's furor rose with each killing. They shrieked with psychotic delight, romping through the blood of their would-be captors. Soon, nearly every soldier lay in a pool of red.

Chapter V

When the few soldiers who managed to escape the bizarre onslaught returned to the castle, they attempted to report the attack, but they were petrified and their accounts made little sense.

"'Tis the dead," one soldier whimpered. "They're, they're coming. They're…"

"Yes, it was… they were undead!" another said. "And painted for war, do you see? War paint! It's… They're back… All those people we killed, all those innocent people we…"

"Oh, God. They're… They've come back for us!"

Disgusted, the Priest-King executed each of the messengers himself and ordered five times the the number of troops to return and capture the Klaun. "BRING ME the HERETICS!" he commanded. "Those HEATHENS will pay for their DEFIANCE!"

Flecky was eager for more blood, and once the clan had spotted the approaching soldiers, he rallied the Klaun warriors for battle. But seeing how outnumbered they were, Jobo knew they stood no chance. To his brother's chagrin, he persuaded the clan to surrender, and they were all taken captive. But as they were being loaded onto the caged prison-carriages, twelve Klaun were randomly pulled from the line, one of whom was Flecky's mother, Olla. Once the cages were locked, the unfortunate dozen were lined up on their knees. Then, one by one, in sight of the whole clan, each of their heads was cut off. Flecky exploded into grief and rage. He set his ire on Jobo, "If we had not SURRENDERED, Mother would be ALIVE!" he cried. "It is YOUR fault, Jobo! You COWARD! You killed Mother! YOU KILLED HER!!!"

Jobo was filled with sorrow. Olla had had a lively, crackling personality, and was a particularly beloved member of the tribe. Jobo adored her as everyone else did, and even regarded her as a second mother. Though he reminded Flecky of this, it was too late. Flecky was indignant and unforgiving. From then on, the bond between the two brothers was broken, and as they split, so too did the tribe.

The heads of the twelve decapitated Klaun were taken ahead of the prison carriages and impaled upon two rows of long pikes leading to the castle gate. Then the captured Klaun were sadistically transported through the ghoulish display and taken to the dungeon.

Chapter VI

It soon became clear to the imprisoned clan that they had been spared death only to be enslaved as performers for the Priest-King's court. At any moment, His Holy Majesty might snap his holy fingers and demand amusement. At these times, a Klaun slave would be taken from the dungeon and quickly costumed to perform. Along with being forced to wear a colorful tight-fitting jumpsuit and curly-toed shoes, the Priest-King further humiliated the performers by forcing them to ironically wear the three-pronged hat that had once symbolized their tribe's freedom. The Priest-King now referred to the Klaun as "jesters" since they were expected to charm their royal audiences with performances of whimsical jest.

If a jester was summoned to entertain before the throne and failed to adequately lighten His Majesty's mood, the jester would be dragged away for torture and decapitation, his or her head then piked and displayed along with the others.

Commanded to smile and perform, the jesters would force big phony grins and desperately attempt to satisfy their audiences. Those not beheaded would be rewarded with mead and table scraps before being returned to the prison. But constantly feigning happiness while being tormented and degraded could only lead to madness.

Chapter VII

With each humiliating jester performance, a Klaun gained some food but lost a piece of themselves. They were filled with intense shame as they grinned and danced like puppets for their master. Those jesters most often chosen to perform began to hate themselves. Fear of torture pushed them on, but not fear of death. The life affirming flame that had once defined the Klaun was now but a flicker, and they hoped only for numbness from the pain of their absurd existence.

Disgusted with what they had become, the jesters' debasement knew no bounds, and they made their performances, costumes, and makeup increasingly ludicrous. They began performing in an imbecilic manner: laughing moronically, bonking themselves on the head, and feigning tripping or clumsily bumping into things.

These self-deprecating performances were a huge success with the royal audiences. They delighted in seeing the Klaun, who had once defied their power and defeated their soldiers, reduced to laughable fools. As they came up with more and more ridiculous costumes, it was permitted to replace the jester uniforms. Many wore garishly bright and ballooning multicolored one-pieces with exaggerated collars and cuffs. They also began to wear grossly oversized shoes, enhancing their clumsy and foolish appearance. The royals now mockingly referred to them as "klowns," a derivation of their tribe's original name, intended to both mock and obscure their people's history.

Lenny: *"So, whoa… this is like, where clowns got to be, kinda like, how they are now, right? Like… that's what you're saying."*

Jesper: *"Well, technically that's what I'm reading, but yeah, I guess you could say that. It's basically the clowning style that caught on later with the masses anyway. But, listen, we'll get to all that later."*

Thick layers of gaudy face-paints served to boggle and amuse the audiences as well as to disguise the klowns' true emotions. Their traditional simple dab of red on the nose became a grotesque splotch covering the entire tip, and they also dyed their hair garish colors. To improve the illusion of cheer, a klown would "put on a happy face" and paint a giant red grin across the mouth. Some added large amounts of blue eye shadow as well. Most importantly, all klowns smeared their skin with the chalky white corpse makeup, as they all felt dead inside.

In addition to entertaining the court, klowns were often called upon for celebrations such as holidays and birthdays. As their spirits were broken through years of torment, security measures were loosened and they were rarely shackled. The Klaun were mere shells of the fearsome warriors that had once laid waste to an entire detachment of soldiers. They were now seen as harmless, silly fools. Klown shows were a particular delight to kids, so they were often used at birthday parties for children of royalty or nobility. To add to their torment, klowns had to endure frequent jeering from the more ill-behaved children. Sometimes these children would shout and throw things at them, or even run up and kick them in the shins and then prance away knowing there would be no reprisal. The Klaun came to despise these cruel spoiled brats.

Chapter VIII

Jobo and Flecky had quickly distinguished themselves as the most entertaining of the Klaun and were frequently summoned to perform together despite their feud. Flecky was very short and wore a ballooning polka dot jumpsuit. He had thick, tightly curled, natural orange hair that crowned his head like a massive carnation. Jobo was tall, lanky, and nearly bald, but maintained a ring of hair around the back of his head that he grew long and dyed bright green. When it was time to perform, Jobo would stretch and glue this green ring of hair to shocking effect, just as he had done for battle years before. With long klown shoes, and a striped tight-fitting jumpsuit, his gangly frame was striking. The brothers captured their audience's attention the moment they leapt on stage, and their showmanship was unmatched.

But over their years of enslavement, ever since the killing of Flecky's mother, the two brothers split farther and farther apart. To endure the suffering of slavery, Jobo became reclusive and turned his mind inward, altering his consciousness to flee his agony. For Flecky, each passing year of slavery and debasement further enflamed the rage that had consumed his heart. He seethed with hate for their royal captors, and some Klaun regarded this abiding anger as strength. Half of the tribe continued to regard Jobo as their chief, no matter how disconnected he became, but the other half gravitated behind Flecky. The clan was divided.

Chapter IX

In the dank dungeon prison, smaller children and elderly Klaun stood little chance of survival. Starvation withered them down to feckless skeletons wrapped in rice paper skin. Dying of hunger and desperate for food, all but Jobo eventually resorted to eating the flesh of those that perished in the dungeon.

Finally feeding upon fresh meat so debauched some of the Klaun that they developed a craving for it and began ravenously eyeing the meek of their tribe. Flecky did not even require the meat, as he was regularly rewarded with scraps when he and Jobo performed, but consuming people's flesh was all that soothed the pain that infected him. It was only after burying his teeth into human flesh and feeling the warmth of its digestion that Flecky could finally take a deep breath and see clearly. His rage was sated and he was momentarily free. He was almost himself again. But when his hunger returned, it was always twice as strong and consumed him with agony.

In his growing madness, Flecky began to conceive of this craving for human flesh as a latent condition in all Klaun. He convinced his followers, the "Fleckers," that all Klaun are born with a natural need for human meat. "Feel not shame for your hunger, nor for the pleasure this meat provides! We have deep within us a hunger that no Klaun can deny—a hunger only satiated by eating this special meat. It is an undesirable condition perhaps, but it is our nature! And it is only by obeying our true nature that we become our true selves."

The rest of the clan, guided by the gentle Jobo, disregarded Flecky's claims. As Flecky preached to his sect that all Klaun were born cannibals, Jobo gathered his group, the "Jobans", into a circle of chants and meditations.

Chapter X

One early morning, after working an all-night festival, Jobo was returned to the dungeon and was met with looks of guilt and disgrace. He learned that during the night, his gravely ill young nephew had died and then been immediately torn from his mother's arms and devoured. Jobo felt a twitch of anger, but crumbled to the ground too crushed by grief to move. Jobo's sister was catatonic, and he neither slept nor left her side for days as he fell into a deep depression and contemplated all of the suffering that the Priest-King had inflicted upon the clan.

During Jobo's dark ruminations, Flecky chattered incessantly into his ear, implanting his cannibalistic vision of the Klaun. On the third day, as Flecky whispered his psychotic beliefs to his brother, he slipped a sliver of dried human flesh into Jobo's mouth. Before he could resist, the nutrients of the meat immediately revived and confused him.

"How can this taste so good?" he wondered. "How can eating this flesh feel so right?" With each satiating bite, Flecky's whisperings made more and more sense to Jobo, and his mind gradually bent to believe that his people, the Klaun, were indeed born cannibals. As he gnawed on the tough dry meat through the night, he was convinced that his hunger must come from a deep inherent need for it. The next day, Jobo finally arose from his trance.

"It is the royals who destroyed our way of life," he intoned. "It is the royals who enslave us. It is the royals who imprison us. It is the royals who torture us. It is the royals who kill us. And it is the royals who must pay. I understand what I am now —what we all are. I know what Klaun require. But this sick priest, this Priest-King, he forces us to feed upon ourselves. To eat our own kin. Our loved ones. Our own children. They make us eat our own children. But I have seen the way, brothers and sisters. I know now what must be done." Jobo's eyes glowed with clarity of purpose. "Finally, the path is clear."

Flecky grinned wide. And as in days long since passed, he rallied the clan behind his brother's plan. He preached Jobo's "righteous vision of retribution" to the Fleckers, infusing them with a sense of vengeful purpose. The Jobans, however, were dejected to see their leader become so maddened by grief. They also craved revenge and escape, but were revolted by his murderous plot.

Chapter XI

The opportunity arrived for Jobo and Flecky to enact the heinous plan when they were summoned for a children's birthday party. The celebration was for a duke's son who was turning seven. Jobo and Flecky were boarded into two small prison-carriages and transported to the event. Upon arriving at their destination, the pair were unloaded and immediately sent to pitch their small dressing tent and prepare themselves.

Birthday celebrations for the children of nobility were extravagant affairs often held outdoors with over a hundred guests in attendance. Various games, lavish buffets, musical entertainment, and a klown show were staple birthday party activities. Royal guards secured the entrance to the expansive party area, but within the gathering there was little regulation. Klown performers were typically allotted a place to pitch one of their small tents to use as a costume changing room and to store props. This benefited Jobo and Flecky in that it gave them a measure of privacy. They found a spot on the outskirts of the great lawn, pitched their tent, and donned their costumes and makeup.

Dozens of royal and noble children attended the celebration. The band struck up a festive tune and soon a carefree merriment pervaded the party. Children scampered about, blowing horns and playing various childhood games as their chaperones absently chatted over pastries, cheeses and fine liqueurs. The two klowns made their rounds, entertaining children and adults alike with their usual routines of juggling, magic, and acrobatic buffoonery.

Jobo knew he had found his mark when he spotted a stout little boy eyeing a shiny, golden, honey-glazed pear on a dessert table reserved for the adults. When the child reached for the forbidden treat, an adult slapped his hand and shooed him away. As the boy vented his frustration by twisting the arm of a smaller child, Jobo crept behind the bully. He bent down and whispered, "A special treat awaits you, my boy. And it is from the grown-ups' table!" With a glance at the pear, Jobo continued, "Shhhh… After dinner, when no one is looking, you must sneak away to the klown tent to claim your prize. But tell no one! Remember, 'tis a secret just for you."

As the picnic dinner was served, Jobo and Flecky swiped a pear and returned to their tiny tent, where they peered through a slit in the canvas and eyed the children. Finally, as dinner was concluding, the boy scurried in their direction. He was a soft spoiled child dressed in silk and velvet, and he clutched a large piece of cake that he had taken from another child at the party. The music started up again and the children began spilling back onto the great lawn to frolic. The boy hunched down at the treed edge of the party area and considered the klown tent as he stuffed himself with cake.

The time had finally come. Jobo and Flecky popped their grinning heads through the tent's flaps. Face covered in frosting, the boy smirked at the two klowns leaning from the tent. Jobo beckoned the child near as Flecky baited him with the coveted golden pear. The gluttonous child glanced toward the shrieking children playing on the lawn, considered how jealous they would be of the forbidden treat, and then bolted for the prize. He lunged for the pear, but Flecky yanked it away and the boy tumbled into the tent.

Jobo sealed the flaps and he and Flecky began giggling like hyenas. The confused child nervously giggled along, but his nervousness turned to fright as the klowns' laughter grew into manic cackles. Suddenly Flecky gagged the child's mouth and tied him to a stool on top of a wide sheet of canvas and Jobo peeked outside to make sure no one was approaching.

The time had come. Jobo staggered for a moment and his hands trembled. Flecky feasted his eyes on the privileged, helpless brat. Gazing maniacally at the boy, Flecky savored every muffled scream. It was the sound of retribution. But Jobo suddenly felt faint. His stomach lurched and the striped tent began to spin. Flecky, meanwhile, with a sadistic grin frozen wide, was entranced by the boy's fear as he slowly approached. He leaned in so close that the child could smell his makeup, feel the hunger in his eyes, and know his intent.

Flecky left the boy's legs fastened to the stool, but slowly untied his wrists. As he released the rope, he noticed a glint of hope in the boy's eyes and burst out laughing as he gripped down hard on the tiny forearms. Then Flecky turned abruptly silent as he stared straight into the child's eyes. He grabbed and squeezed each of the child's

small palms, extending the plump little fingers, which he brought to his lips. Teasingly, he mock-nibbled on the tender morsels as he gazed at the trembling boy.

"NOM nom nom nom nommm…" Flecky taunted, "I'm gonna eat youuuu. NOM nom nom nom nom nom nommm. I'm gonna eat you UP!"

The terrified child was shocked to silence. Flecky stopped, turned to Jobo and whispered, "Showtime."

His eyes flashed wildly at Jobo, inviting him to grab hold onto one of the child's plump arms. This was the moment of revenge Jobo had imagined, but with the opportunity finally in front of him, he was struck with vertigo and regret. The tent was spinning and his ears rang as darkness encroached into his vision. Just as Jobo lost consciousness, he saw Flecky's teeth sink down into the boy's forearm, a flash of a bloody smile, a drip from a chin. He was eating the boy alive.

Flecky then gnawed off one of the boy's fingers and teased his gagging, squealing victim, "Ohhh, quiet down now. It'll all be over soon. As soon as I'm done eating this, I'll just slit your thr-*GLLRRF!*"

Jobo grabbed Flecky by the neck and slammed him to the ground. He pressed a knee down hard into Flecky's chest as he leaned over him and croaked, "STOP, Flecky! It's not… This is WRONG!"

Jobo stood and Flecky gasped and choked as he got up and then mumbled indignantly while wiping the blood from his face and hands. He put on a new costume and reapplied his white makeup. Then he defiantly picked up the bloody finger, dabbed his nose with it, and painted a red frown across his mouth, disguising his smug grin.

Both of the klowns then rolled the child up inside the sheet of canvas, with Jobo making sure the barely conscious boy was silenced but able to breathe. They collapsed their tent with the canvas bundle hidden inside, and loaded everything into the prison-carriages. They gave a quick final performance for the partygoers, and then bounded across the lawn and into the backs of the wooden carriages for a dramatic exit. The soldiers locked them in and headed back to the dungeon. Jobo tended to the boy as best he could during the trip back, but he was losing blood fast.

Chapter XII

That night, hearing the prison-carriages return to the dungeon, the Klaun gathered into position behind the iron cell door. As the latch was released, they barreled through, slamming the two unsuspecting soldiers to the ground. They pounced upon the soldiers, dragged them into the cell, and chopped off their heads with their own swords. Jobo and Flecky then donned the dead soldiers' armor and took their weapons.

When Jobo dragged the tent into a corner of the dungeon and unraveled it, the boy was barely alive, and the Jobans immediately encircled the child to protect him from Flecky's encroaching cult. Just as the two Klaun factions were about to battle, the boy gurgled his final breath. With no life left to protect, the Jobans relented and the Fleckers snatched the the dead child away. They brought the body over to Flecky and lined up in front of him as he quickly sliced small pieces from the fresh corpse. Then, as was originally planned, he ceremoniously presented a bloody sliver to each of the Fleckers and asked, "Do you swear to consume only the flesh of your oppressor?"

"I do," each Flecker vowed in turn and swallowed the meat.

Jobo was anguished that the boy had not survived. He had come to his senses too late to save him and the Fleckers got their ritual after all. He knew there would eventually be a reckoning between the two Klaun sides, but the only thing to do now was escape the dungeon as quickly as possible and find safety for the Jobans.

As all of the Klaun gathered at the door, Jobo swung up his sword, "Klaun! Dawn approaches! We must all step from this tomb and return to life! We go our separate ways, yes, but we are all Klaun, and from now on, the Klaun lineage must be kept secret. Our descendants shall never face such persecution again! And tonight, on this night, finally all Klaun are FREE!"

The Jobans cheered in support, and Flecky concurred with his brother, "Indeed! Tonight all Klaun are freed from this wretched hole and returned to the world. And of course the bloodline of our people must forever be guarded from outsiders. But in time," he pointed at the Jobans, "all Klaun must feed." As all the Fleckers roared for their leader, Jobo directed his group to the door.

Then, at long last, all of the pale emaciated Klaun prisoners staggered out into the moonlight. The two small prison-carriages were not big enough to hold either group, but they shoved themselves in. One by one, they desperately contorted their bodies and folded themselves into the tiny carriages, filling them to their roofs with every last Klaun. Once they had all piled in, Jobo and Flecky took the reins, and the two Klaun carriages escaped into the night.

— The End —

Epilogue

Jesper gently closes the book, pushes his long stringy grey hair from his face, and raises his eyes to mine. I hold up my glass, which he clinks with his own, and we down what's left of our scotch. He pours the last of the bottle into my glass. Then he fixes another stare on me, but this time his eyes are wide and soft. He looks like he's about to apologize. And then it clicks—he had seemed vaguely familiar up to that moment, but now I know where I've seen him before.

Lenny: *"All those years, when I was younger, when I was a kid, that was you, wasn't it."* (I'm not really asking - I know.) *"But you were always at a distance. Yeah, you even waved at me once, the last time, when you knew I'd spotted you, ...while we were driving away. It's just that it's been so long! It's been years. And you grew a beard, and you don't have your makeup on. That's what was throwing me off! Plus, you're a lot... You used to be so skinny! Oh my God! All this time... I thought I was nuts! I thought maybe I was hallucinating or something,* *seeing that same goddamned clown pop up again and again all those years! Sometimes performing, sometimes just in a crowd or down the street… but it was always that SAME FUCKING CLOWN! That same one! It was always YOU, wasn't it?!"*

Suddenly I feel an acute need to get away and I shoot from my chair, but I'm too drunk and my head sways, so I lean forward and hold onto the table. *"Why did you… What do you want? Who… What is this?"* I fall back into my seat.

Jesper: He seems ashamed as he fumbles for words, and his eyes are bleary. *"Yes, that was me, Lenny. I was looking out for you is all. I… I just needed to see how you were doing, …and your mother."*

Lenny: *"How do you…"*

Jesper: *"After… When your father died, I had to… I had to keep an eye on you, Lenny. So I was…"*

Lenny: *"Wait, WHAT? What the… How do you know about my father?"*

Jesper: He pulls a white envelope from his coat, shakes it at me and says, *"Read this. It'll explain everything and tell you where to find me. I'm sorry, Lenny."* Then he tucks the letter into the leather storybook, which he sets in front of me as he gets up and says, *"This book, it's yours now, whatever you* *decide."* He pauses next to me as he leaves and grips my shoulder, *"Lenny. The Fleckers... They know who you are."*

**Letter to Lenore Watts
from Jesper the Klaun**:

Dear Lenny,

There is so much to tell you. Let me begin by picking up where the story of the Klaun leaves off. We'll start with that. I'll try to tell you in a nutshell what's happened since then.

After their escape, the Klaun quietly spread throughout Europe and other parts of the world. They survived however they could, often working as street performers, all while preserving their Klaun heritage and keeping their ancestry secret. Ironically, keeping their history a secret was actually made easier by the Priest-King. Pissed off and humiliated by the tribe's escape, he banned their name and made even uttering "Klaun/klown" punishable by death.

In time, the Klaun invented the word "clown" to market their abilities to theater companies while

89

*still essentially hiding the long forgotten Klaun
name. They were a success, and were eventually
hired from these theaters to join the first circuses.
Clowns quickly became so indispensable in the
circus circuit that the term "clown" became
synonymous with circuses. No circus was complete
without a troupe of clowns, so when there weren't
enough true Klaun to go around, circus owners
improvised. They started putting regular people in
makeup and calling them clowns, too.*

*Around the start of the 19th century,
traveling circuses gained popularity throughout the
United States, and many Fleckers immigrated to the
States, with the Jobans trailing close after them.*

*Joining carnivals and traveling circuses,
finally the Klaun had returned to their nomadic
performer roots. Sure, they weren't treated great, but
they were more or less regarded as human beings,
which was a step up from what many of them were
used to. The American circus life suited them well
and Klaun numbers steadily grew in the States. But
it was no coincidence that child kidnapping and
murder statistics grew as well. Constant relocation
from town to town with circuses meant that the*

descendants of Flecky's sect were able to time their killings and relocate often before police could even launch an investigation. And, anyway, the local cops usually suspected visiting carnival goers from nearby towns whenever children would go missing from carnival crowds. They certainly didn't suspect the seemingly jolly clowns of any malevolence.

Of course, today most professional clowns are not dangerous, and are actually completely oblivious to the existence of the Klaun tribe. Lots of them are just theatrical types who genuinely love kids. For centuries, professional clowns have been kept unaware as they've performed and sometimes lived alongside actual Klaun. But the Jobans and Fleckers have been in a clandestine war with each other all along. We Klaun have closely guarded our family tree for centuries. We took a vow of secrecy, on both sides. Even the handful of Fleckers who were caught by the authorities (a few infamous murderers I need not name) never used to leak our secret Klaun lineage.

Each Klaun generation has dutifully passed down our people's traditions to the next. But for descendants of Flecky's sect, these traditions have *also included abduction and ritualized cannibalism of children born to the social elite. The Jobans meanwhile, my clan, have always devoted ourselves to protecting children, no matter what their class, especially from the Fleckers. We hunt them down, Lenny. The Jobans have been quietly hunting Fleckers for centuries. It is the duty of each new generation of Jobans to quietly continue this work until the Fleckers are stopped.*

It's hard to believe, but the Fleckers actually say that we are unfairly persecuting them for being true to what they say is the Klaun's true nature. They are convinced that all Klaun somehow require human meat, so they only consider one to be full Klaun once he or she has eaten it. And they even consider themselves righteous for only eating what they call "the flesh of the oppressor" since they target the privileged children of the rich and powerful.

But we've failed, Lenny. The Jobans have failed, after all these years, to stamp these sickos out. And now their numbers grow every day. We thought we could stop them. We always thought we were so close to the end. And a few years ago, we actually were. We had them. But then they started doing something unheard of - something no Klaun generation ever did before. They started recruiting. They're recruiting non-Klaun, or "norms" as we call them. And the police, parents, everybody—they have no idea about any of this. No one understands what's coming.

The Fleckers broke the code. So now all bets are off. With these norm recruits, Flecker numbers are increasing exponentially, and they are bolder than ever. Plus, there's no doubt that the Fleckers have been spilling our Klaun secrets, including our origin story to all those norm recruits, so the public is going to hear it all anyway, one way or the other. A lot of Jobans don't agree with me, but I say we have to at least try to get the word out, to publish our story, and give the people a fighting chance.

But getting the word out isn't really the main reason I contacted you, Lenny. I came to you first for another reason. You see, you need to know that the Fleckers have known about you all your life. This is because you are Klaun, Lenny. Your mother was a norm, but your father was a Flecker. I understand this will be hard to swallow, but it is the truth.

Lenny, you are Klaun. So you are a part of all this whether you like it or not. I'm sorry.

They will be coming for you now, and when they do, they will treat you with all the affection of a long-lost daughter, which you sort of are. They will make you feel like a princess and tell you all sorts of lies to get you to join them. But if you refuse, Lenny, they will cut your throat. Have no illusions about this. Once they have exposed their Flecker identities to you, there is absolutely no way they will allow you to continue living without pledging your loyalty and joining them.

Lenny, I want you to know that your dad never told your mom that he was Klaun, let alone a Flecker. She didn't know. Not only was your mom a norm, but she was a sweet lady, and I can promise you she never knew your father was a killer. That day at your house, when I finally caught up with your father, you were eight years old. I had identified him as the murderer of a toddler found dead in the local mountains. The boy's body was actually found charred on a spit over what had been your father's campfire.

I'm sorry Lenny, but your father was a sick man. As bad as they come. So, I ended him. I'm sorry you saw what you did. I didn't mean for you to see it happen. I thought you weren't home that day. But he was a Flecker and you have to understand that when Fleckers have children with norms, the result is always the same. At some point before the child's tenth birthday, they always murder the norm parent. Always. That way when the kid hits ten years old, they are free to raise him or her as a Flecker.

I paid your uncles a visit once your father was gone, and let's just say I made them promise to leave you and your mother alone after that. She would raise you as a norm, all of us Klaun would stay out of your life, and that would be that.

Your mom was a good lady and she did her best to raise you, but as you know, she was never the same after all that. So I kept checking up on you to make sure the Fleckers didn't suck you in and make you one of them. I also wanted to make sure they weren't going to hurt your mother.

Over the years, I had to give your uncles a few reminders of their promise. And by "reminders" I mean broken appendages. I guess ever since that day you saw me and your dad, I've felt responsible for you. It was traumatic for you, I know, and I'm sorry it went that way. I'm sorry you saw that. It wasn't the plan. After that, I just wanted to make sure you turned out all right.

The Fleckers finally got the message and have kept their distance since then. But I can't hold them off any longer. With the whole recruitment push the Fleckers are doing, they are set on finding you again and bringing you into the fold. They say a great battle is coming, so they are looking for every possible soldier, especially ones with true Klaun blood like you. I'm sorry it's come to this.

There is no running from this, Lenny. You've been part of the Klaun war since the day you were born; you just never knew it. I kept telling myself I could keep you from it, but I think deep down I always knew this day would come. Now that I've told you the secret story of your ancestors, you are finally what we call a "realized" Klaun. You see, each Klaun parent or guardian transcribes the story into a book, reads it to their child on the eve of their tenth birthday, and then gives it to him or her. This is exactly what I have done for you today, Lenny. Twenty years late, sure, but I've done it. So now you're finally realized. You are officially initiated. So keep this book safe. It's yours.

Yes, your relatives are Fleckers, Lenny, and they will be coming to claim you, but the choice is not theirs. It's yours. Nobody owns you, Lenny. The way I see it at this point is that you are just Klaun. Not Flecker, not Joban, just Klaun. I mean the Klaun were around before Jobo and Flecky anyway, so you're Klaun, Lenny. That much is for sure. But you have a choice that few Klaun have ever had before. You can decide for yourself which side you are on. Of course this shouldn't be a tough call, the Fleckers are goddamned psychopaths, but the they will try to confuse you and convince you that you belong with them. Plus, once they find you, they really won't leave you much choice. Just remember the Jobans will have your back if you join us.

And yes, I'm aware that you've become quite the thief. I was upset about this at first, but the truth is that this skill will make you an immediate asset to *whoever you join. It's your call to make though. It's your decision. Do what you must. But again, let me be clear that this is a decision you cannot delay. They will be coming for you any day now.*

I really am sorry for all this, Lenny. I know you've been battling some demons, and I know I've been one of them. But I do think together we might be able to fix some things. If you decide to join the Jobans, meet me at Luna Park this Saturday at dawn in front of the Cyclone. I will teach you all I can.

- Jesper

20716107R00060